Written by
Dori Hillestad Butler

Illustrated by
Nancy Meyers

PEACHTREE
ATLANTA

For my mom, and in memory of my dad,
who inspired my interest in codes

—D. H. B.

For Danny, Emma, Grace, and Sullivan,
who inspire me every day

—N. M.

Published by
PEACHTREE PUBLISHING COMPANY INC.
1700 Chattahoochee Avenue
Atlanta, Georgia 30318-2112
www.peachtree-online.com

First trade paperback edition published in 2018

Edited by Kathy Landwehr
Design and composition by Nicola Simmonds Carmack
The illustrations were drawn in pencil with color added digitally.

Printed in August 2020 by Toppan Leefung Printing Limited in China
10 9 8 7 6 5 4 (hardcover)
10 9 8 7 6 5 (trade paperback)

HC ISBN: 978-1-56145-878-3
PB ISBN: 978-1-68263-016-7

Library of Congress Cataloging-in-Publication Data

Names: Butler, Dori Hillestad, author. | Meyers, Nancy, 1961– illustrator.
Title: King and Kayla and the case of the secret code / written by Dori Hillestad Butler ; illustrated by Nancy Meyers.
Description: First edition. | Atlanta GA : Peachtree Publishers, [2017] | Summary: When a mysterious letter written in code arrives at King's house for his human, Kayla, he follows the trail of the person who left it.
Identifiers: LCCN 2016020442 | ISBN 9781561458783
Subjects: | CYAC: Dogs—Fiction. | Ciphers—Fiction. | Mystery and detective stories.
Classification: LCC PZ7.B9759 Kis 2017 | DDC [E]—dc23 LC record available at *https://lccn.loc.gov/2016020442*

Contents

Chapter One

Ding-dong!

Hello!

My name is King. I'm a dog.

This is Kayla. She is my human.

I'm trying to teach Kayla a new trick. It's called the Get King Some Cheese Trick. I LOVE cheese. It's my favorite food!

Here's how the trick works:

I go to the refrigerator.

I sit.

I say, "Please get me some cheese."

Kayla is having a hard time learning this trick.

I say it louder: "PLEASE GET ME SOME CHEESE!"

"Don't bark, King," Kayla says.

I'm not barking. I'm just trying to teach Kayla a new trick.

But she doesn't understand.

I try singing. "Let's go to the refrigerator! Let's get King some cheese!"

I dance around the kitchen.

“Ohhhh, I get it,” Kayla says. “You want to go outside.”

“No! I don’t want to go outside,” I say. Why do humans always think dogs want to go outside?

Ding-dong!

"Someone's here! Someone's here!" I say. Kayla and I race to the door.

"Who's there?" Kayla asks. She peeks out the window. Then she opens the door.

I crowd in beside her to see who it is.

My tail droops.

No one is there.

Chapter Two

The Letter

There's a letter on our doormat. I pick it up and give it to Kayla.

"Thank you, King," she says with a smile.

628
Kayla

We go back inside. Kayla opens the letter. Her smile disappears. “I can’t read this,” she says.

Cdzq Jzxkz,

Bnld sn z Rdbqds Rox Ozqsx.

Lx gntrd.

Rzstqczx zs mnnm.

Knud, Ihkkhzm

"There aren't any vowels in most of the words," Kayla says. "You can't make words without vowels."

I don't know what vowels are.

And these are the only words I know how to read:

K-A-Y-L-A

K-I-N-G

V-E-T

P-O-U-N-D.

None of those words are in Kayla's letter.

“Who would leave a strange letter on our doormat?” Kayla asks.

Sniff…sniff… The paper smells like oatmeal. I LOVE oatmeal. It’s my favorite food!

It also smells like Kayla’s friend Jillian.

Ding-dong!

"Someone's here! Someone's here!" I say. Kayla and I race to the door.

Is it Jillian?

Kayla peeks out the window. Then she opens the door. It's not Jillian. It's Mason. I LOVE Mason. He's my favorite boy!

I hop up and kiss him all over.

"No, King," Kayla says.

Oops. I forgot Kayla doesn't like it when I kiss other humans.

“Someone rang my doorbell and ran away,” Mason tells Kayla. “Was it you?”

“No,” she says. “Someone rang my doorbell and ran away, too. They left a letter, but I can’t read it.”

“I got a letter, too,” Mason says. “I can’t read my letter, either.”

Kayla and Mason put their letters side by side.

Cdzq, Jzxkz,

Bnld sn z Rdbqds Rox Ozqsx.

Lx gntrd.

Rzstqczx zs mnnm.

Knud, Ihkkhzm

"They're almost exactly the same," Kayla says. "The second word is the only one that's different."

Cdzq Lzrnm,

Bnld sn z Rdbqds Rox Ozqsx.

Lx gntrd

Rzstqczx zs mnnm.

Knud, Ihkkhzm

"That doesn't help," Mason says. "We don't know what any of the words say."

Chapter Three

Making Lists

"Who would leave us letters that we can't read?" Mason asks.

Sniff...sniff... Mason's letter smells like Jillian, too.

"I think Jillian left the letters," I say. But Kayla and Mason don't understand me.

"It must be someone we both know," Kayla says.

"Jillian," I say again.

Kayla looks at me. "Do you need to go outside, King?"

"No!" I say. "I'm trying to tell you who left the letters."

"Why would someone leave us letters that we can't read?" Mason asks.

"Maybe it's a game," Kayla says. "Maybe it's supposed to be fun. Like solving a mystery."

"It's a mystery alright," Mason says. "But I don't know how to solve a mystery."

"I do," Kayla says.

She grabs a notebook and pencil. "Let's make a list of everything we *know* about this case," she says.

1. The same person left both letters.
2. It's someone we both know.
3. The two letters are the same, except for the second word.

If I could write, I would add this to Kayla's list of things we know:

“Now let’s make a list of what we *don’t know* about this case,” Kayla says.

1. Who sent the letters?
2. What do the letters say?
3. How do we figure out what the letters say?

If I could write, I would add this to Kayla's list of things we don't know:

"Now we need a *plan,*" Kayla says.

I have a plan:

Chapter Four

King's Plan

I run to the door. "I need to go outside! I need to go outside!" I shout.

"I think King needs to go outside," Kayla tells Mason.

"Yes! Yes! Yes!" I dance around to show her that I really do want to go outside this time.

Kayla grabs my leash and snaps it to my collar. Then we all go outside.

Sniff…sniff… I smell Jillian's scent. It's on our front porch. It's on our front steps. It's on our sidewalk.

Kayla holds tight to my leash. "Slow down, King," she says.

But I can't slow down. I've got Jillian's scent!

I follow Jillian's scent down the street. Kayla and Mason have to run to keep up.

I follow Jillian's scent around the corner.

"King!" Kayla yells. "Slow down! I mean it!" She pulls on my leash.

But I pull harder. I pull the leash right out of Kayla's hand.

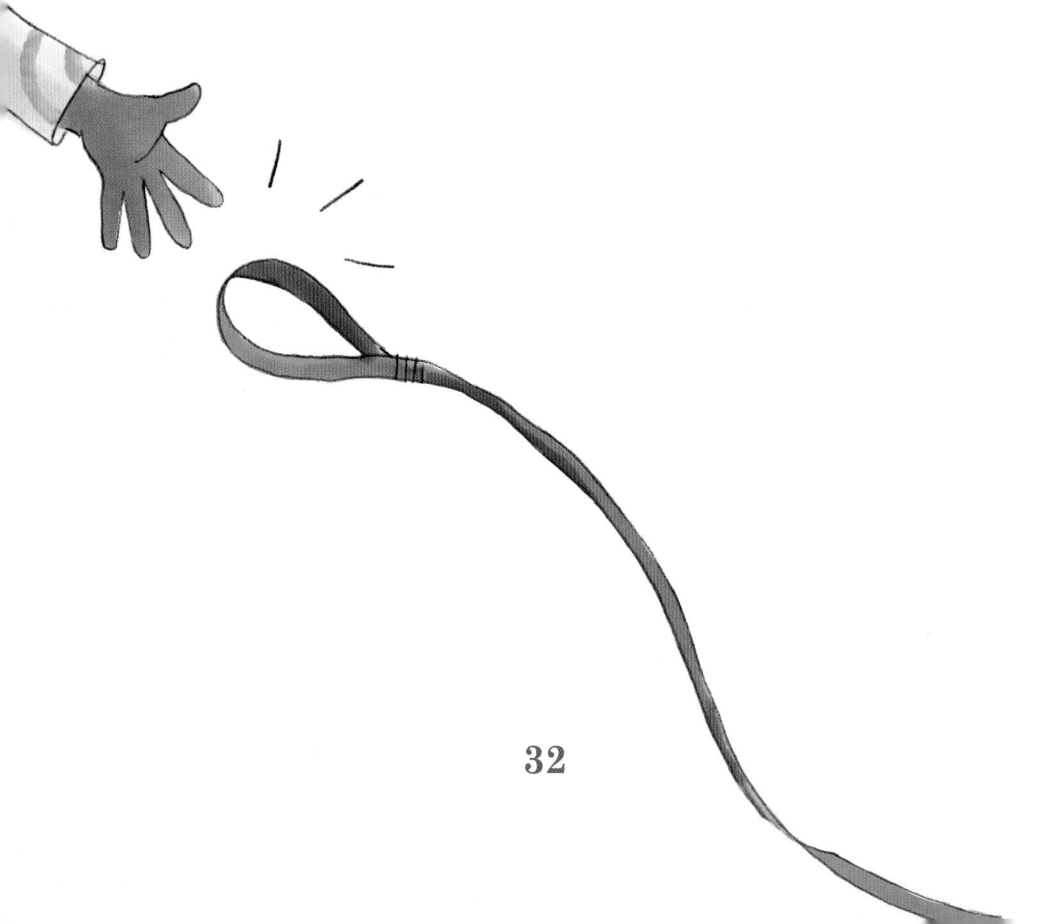

“Come back here, King!” Kayla screams. She stomps her foot. “You are being a bad dog!”

I stop. I don’t like it when Kayla says I’m a bad dog.

But then I see Jillian!

She is only eleventy ten houses away.

"I'm not a bad dog," I tell Kayla. "I'm a good dog. You'll see. I'm going to help you solve this case!"

I run toward Jillian.

Kayla sees Jillian, too. “Help, Jillian!” she screams. “King is loose! Help me catch him!”

Jillian turns. She runs toward me.

I let her catch me!

Guess what? She's got another one of those letters in her hand. It looks just like the letters she left for Kayla and Mason.

Asia

Chapter Five

Cracking the Code

Kayla grabs my leash. “Thanks, Jillian,” she says.

“What’s that in your hand?” Mason asks Jillian.

Jillian puts the letter behind her back. But it’s too late. Kayla and Mason have already seen it.

"It's a letter for Asia," Jillian says. "I need to drop it off at her house."

"It looks like the letters we found on our front porches," Mason says.

"Did you leave letters on our porches?" Kayla asks.

Jillian blushes. "Yes," she says.

"But we can't read them," Mason says.

"That's because they're written in code," Jillian says. "You have to crack the code."

"How?" Mason asks.

"I'll give you a hint," Jillian says. "*Z* equals *A*."

"What kind of hint is that?" Mason asks.

Jillian just smiles and walks away.

We go back to our house. Kayla and Mason put their letters on the kitchen table.

“Let’s change all the Z’s in our letters to A’s,” Kayla says.

Cdzq Jzxkz,

Bnld sn z Rdbqds Rox Ozqsx.

Lx gntrd.

Rzstqczx zs mnnm.

Knud, Ihkkhzm

"That looks better," Mason says.

"Yes, because now we have more vowels," Kayla says.

Cdzq Lzrnm,

Bnld sn z Rdbqds Rox Ozqsx.

Lx gntrd

Rzstqczx zs mnnm.

Knud, Ihkkhzm

"The words still don't look like real words," Mason says.

"If *Z* equals *A*, then maybe *A* equals *B*," Kayla says.

"And maybe *B* equals *C*. And *C* equals *D*," Mason says.

"Let's change all the letters to the next one in the alphabet," Kayla says.

After a little while, Kayla says, “I know what the first line says!”

“Me too,” Mason says. “‘Dear Mason.’”

“Mine says ‘Dear Kayla,’” Kayla says.

They read the rest together:

Cdzq, Jzxkz,
Dear Kayla,

Bnld sn z Rdbqds Rox Ozqsx.
Come to a Secret Spy Party.

Lx gntrd.
My house.

Rzstqczx zs mnnm.
Saturday at noon.

Knud, Ihkkhzm
Love, Jillian

"Hooray! We cracked the code!" Kayla says.

Now maybe they can crack my code.

I go to the refrigerator. I sit. I say, "Please get me some cheese."

"What's the matter, King?" Kayla asks. "Do you need to go outside?"

I groan.

"I know what he wants," Mason says. He walks over to me.

Oh, boy! Oh, boy! I'm going to get some cheese!

He picks up my ball. "I think King wants to play fetch!"

Close enough!
I LOVE to play fetch.
It's my favorite thing!

The End

Oh, boy! I LOVE books. They're my favorite things!

More great mysteries from
King & Kayla

King and Kayla and the Case of the Missing Dog Treats

HC: $14.95 / 978-1-56145-877-6
PB: $6.95 / 978-1-68263-015-0

When some fresh-baked dog treats disappear, King sniffs out the clues to help Kayla find out what happened to them.

"A great introduction to mysteries, gathering facts, and analytical thinking for an unusually young set."
—*Booklist*

King & Kayla and the Case of the Mysterious Mouse

HC: $14.95 / 978-1-56145-879-0

When King's favorite blue ball goes missing, he and Kayla must put together clues to figure out where it went—and who has it.

"Confusion, mischief, and silliness abound."
—*Kirkus Reviews*

King & Kayla and the Case of the Lost Tooth

HC: $14.95 / 978-1-56145-880-6

Kayla lost a tooth—but now it's missing. Where did it go?

"This funny, endearing addition to the series will delight early readers, especially dog lovers."
—*Kirkus Reviews*